Molly's Jolly Brolly

By
Erica-Jane
Waters

meadowside
CHILDREN'S BOOKS

It was a rainy day and Molly decided to go for a walk with her new brolly.

On her way out she met Bobby,
the boy next door.
"What a jolly brolly,"
said Bobby.

"This is no ordinary brolly," said Molly.

"My brolly and I have…

"...zoomed to the moon,
where we saw a rocket ship
and we searched for little
green moon men."

Molly walked to the park to see the ducks.

"What a jolly brolly," said the park keeper.

"This is no ordinary brolly," said Molly.

"My brolly and I have...

"…sailed the seas,
where we met some pirates
and had tea and cake
on their ship."

Molly and her brolly sat down
next to a little old lady.
"What a jolly brolly,"
said the old lady.

"This is no ordinary brolly," said Molly.
"My brolly and I have...

"...flown through
the clouds
to a magic castle,
deep in the woods
where I was princess for a day."

Molly went to see Mr Green
in the Sweetie Shop.
"What a jolly brolly," said Mr Green.

"This is no ordinary brolly," said Molly.

"My brolly and I have…

"...sailed down the cherryade river
to the land of sweets, where
the hills are made of jelly
and I munched and chewed
'til my tummy was full."

When Molly and her brolly
got home, Mum asked,
"Where have you been?"

"Oh just for a walk," said Molly,

"Just me...

"...and my brolly!"

For Mum and Dad,
With all my love

E.J.W.

First published in 2006
by Meadowside Children's Books
185 Fleet Street
London EC4A 2HS

A CIP catalogue record for this book
is available from the British Library

ISBN 10 pbk 1-84539-188-8
ISBN 13 pbk 978-1-84539-188-1
ISBN 10 hbk 1-84539-189-6
ISBN 13 hbk 978-1-84539-189-8

10 9 8 7 6 5 4 3 2 1
Printed in China

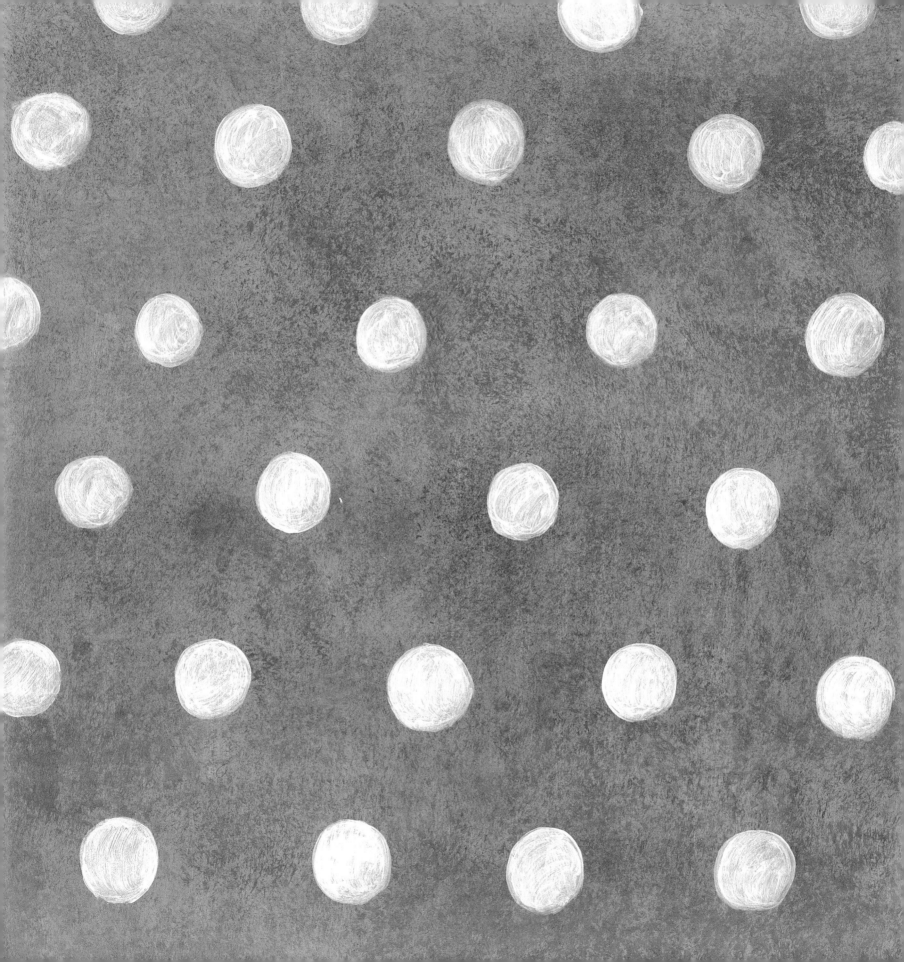